THE MURDER IN THE DRESSING ROOM

BAKERS AND BULLDOG MURDERS

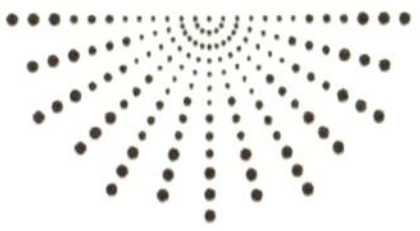

ROSIE SAMS

The Murder in the Dressing Room

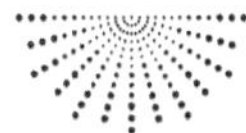

The morning was bright and cheery, and the last remnants of winter had finally left the cozy little seaside town of Port Warren. Melody had gotten up nice and early and was ready for the day ahead.

In the kitchen, a little bundle of joy bounced up and down on all four paws. Called a blue and white, because her dark grey coat looked blue, Smudge was happy to be moving. Melody snapped the leash onto the faithful puppy's collar, and the pair set off to work.

Taking the scenic route, she and Smudge had sauntered along, basking in all of the sights and sounds that the first days of spring had to offer. The snow had finally melted, tiny green shoots could be found pushing their way up through the fresh earth, and a few birds had made their return from down south and were gleefully singing their morning songs. Smudge pranced along ahead, tail wagging, leading the way to Decadently Delicious. This was the award-winning bakery that Melody had opened a few years earlier. Being the skilled pastry chef that she was, it was no surprise that the bakery was thriving. New orders came in daily, and there was always a steady stream of people coming and going, picking up their favorite desserts to bring home for a tasty after-dinner treat.

Fumbling with her keys, Melody unlocked the front door to the shop, stepped inside and switched on the lights, ready to get to work. She went back to the kitchen, turned on all of the ovens, and did a quick inventory check to ensure that all of the necessary supplies and ingredients were on hand to fulfill the day's orders. Everything was set and ready to go. The only things missing were her two assistants. As she pulled up her sleeve to check her watch, she heard the front door chimes ring. Seconds later, Kerry Porter, her first assistant came bouncing into the back.

"You'll never guess what I did last night, Mel!" Kerry started in her normal exuberant way. She always spoke so fast that no one could get a word in edgeways. It looked like this morning was no exception. "It was absolutely wonderful! Bradford took me out for the most romantic dinner at the new steakhouse downtown, and then after dinner we spent the rest of the evening dancing. We spun around the room in each other's arms. It was absolutely magical!" Kerry was swooning and pretending to dance around the shop. It seemed that her relationship with Bradford was recovering nicely from some of the hardships that it had gone through in its early days.

Melody laughed. "I'm really happy for you, Ker. I'm so glad that after all that you and Bradford have been through, things are finally working out. Just remember," she gestured to her watch, tapping its glass face, "I can't have you letting your personal relationships get in the way of work. You're ten minutes late already. We could have had the first batch of cakes mixed and ready to go into the oven by now."

Nodding at Melody, Kerry agreed. "You're totally right, Mel, I'm really sorry. I got off to a late start this morning. I swear it will never happen again." Kerry took a quick look around. "At least I'm here earlier than Leslie. Where is she anyway? It's not like her to be this tardy."

"Your right, Kerry, she is usually pretty punctual." Melody sighed, where was that girl? "We have a ton of orders to complete today. I'd better give her a call and find out what's going on."

Melody pulled out her cell phone and dialed Leslie's number, but there was no answer. Hanging up she tried again, and again. Finally, with no joy, she left a message for Leslie to return her call or come into the bakery as soon as possible. Melody turned to Kerry. "No answer," she said. "It's strange, but I'm sure she will show up. We'd better not waste any more time, or else no one will be getting their treats today."

Halfway through their second batch of double chocolate fudge cupcakes, Leslie came running in, startling Smudge out of a quick nap and causing the pup to start up into a round of barking. The girl was out of breath and had apparently run the whole way from her home to the bakeshop.

Kerry put a hand on Smudge's head to reassure her

and to bring some calm to the chaotic situation that Leslie had created. "Well, good morning!" Kerry joked, considering it was nearly the afternoon. "Where have you been? We've been here slaving away, trying to pick up your slack."

"I'm so sorry, guys," Leslie apologized, looking sincerely upset.

Melody walked over, wiping her hands on her apron, and was interested to hear what kind of excuse Leslie had for her late arrival.

Leslie looked a little embarrassed but sort of glowing at the same time. "I actually think I have a new calling, guys! I mean, don't get me wrong, I'll never give up baking, but I met someone yesterday afternoon, and he's opened up my eyes to a whole new world of possibilities!"

Melody and Kerry looked at each other quizzically and then back at Leslie, waiting for her to continue.

"I was at the market, picking up some groceries when I dropped an orange. It rolled away, down the aisle, and as I was chasing it, I bumped right into Jamison Shepherd. He's from New York, and he's acting as the guest director for the Port Warren playhouse. He has been involved in so many productions with plenty of famous actors and actresses, and he has a ton of amazing stories." Leslie clasped her hands together and closed her eyes as if reliving the meeting. "We hit it off right away. We went out for a few drinks and then dinner and ended up staying up almost all night discussing writing and art and the meaning of life." Leslie had a faraway look in her eyes as she spoke.

"I see," Kerry said, trying to hide the smirk on her face. "So, you're in love? You've got the hots for this fancy new director?"

Leslie's face turned bright red at Kerry's remarks. "No!" She exclaimed, perhaps a little too loudly. "It's not like that. I mean, he's a great guy and all, but I'm just really looking forward to auditioning for the play. Jamison thinks I'll make a great actress."

"I think that's really nice, Leslie," Melody said, putting a hand on the girl's shoulder. "You're going to have a wonderful time, but you have to make sure that you keep your priorities straight and get to work on time. We need your help here. Also, be careful of this Jamison guy. He's new to town and comes from the big city. Things are a lot different out there.

Make sure you keep your head about you until you get to know him a little better. You never know what someone's intentions may be."

Leslie vowed that she would be vigilant on both fronts. "I won't be late again, Mel, this was a one-time mistake, I swear. I'll be careful of Jamison as well, but I promise you, he's a really great guy, you guys are going to adore him!" And with that she quickly threw on an apron and set to work, baking up a batch of macaroons.

Melody shook her head and sighed, setting off towards her office with Smudge at her heels. There was never a dull moment at Decadently Delicious.

CHAPTER TWO

Spending an afternoon driving around town and taking in all of the sights was always one of the best ways to get a feel for a place and to find the hidden gems that a town was hiding. The flamboyant and black-haired Jamison Shepherd had gotten up early that morning and was intent on figuring out just what the tiny town of Port Warren was all about. He had had a feeling since the moment he had set foot in town that it would be the perfect location for his next play. It was the complete opposite of Manhattan, where he had been building up his directing career over the years.

If I'm careful here and play all of my cards right, I'll be the hottest thing that New York has ever seen. I'll have actresses on their knees, begging me to cast them. My name will be in lights all over the city. Jamison had always been a dreamer. One who was motivated by fame and fortune and his dreams were running wild in his head as he cruised the quiet streets.

Since New York was such an expensive city, Jamison had begun to move some of his productions to smaller towns around the country. It gave him the perfect opportunity to showcase his directing talents and spread his name, without incurring the astronomical costs associated with a Broadway production. He figured that this would be the last small town gig he would need. After this, everyone in the business would know of his top-notch directing reputation, and getting the funding required for the big city shows would be a breeze.

Luckily enough, the weather was warm, and he was able to drive with the top of his bright red, sporty convertible down. It was drawing looks from all of those that he passed, and Jamison soaked in every minute of it. Expertly squeezing into a tiny, street-side spot on Main Street, he locked the doors and threw his hands into his pockets. He was determined to find inspiration for his new production and source out all of the things he would need for the show to run smoothly.

Port Warren was a cute town, he mused. Small town America with nothing particularly special or unique about it. Passing a little bakery, he made a note to himself to talk to the head baker about the possibility of catering for his cast and crew.

Across the street was a small tailor shop. *Someone there may be able to help me with costume fittings and alterations.* He took a mental note. He also noted the interesting looks he was getting from those that he passed in the street. *Perhaps they don't get many outsiders here,* he laughed to himself. Or perhaps it was his bright green, pinstriped suit, black slicked-back hair, and a black mustache that was drawing all of the attention. He definitely wasn't what Port Warren was used to.

Rounding the next corner to head towards the waterfront, Jamison stopped in awe. Tucked back, almost out of view from the sidewalk, was an art gallery. The large, floor-to-ceiling windows displayed some of the most beautiful paintings he had ever seen. The quality was just like something that he would have found in the city, if not much, much better.

Bursting into the front door, Jamison's loud and somewhat abrasive voice rang out. "I need to speak to someone immediately! Service, please, service!"

From out of the back room, a handsome, young man walked up slowly wearing paint-splattered blue jeans. Wiping his hands on an old rag and tossing it over his shoulder he looked at the boisterous man who was making a ruckus in his shop.

"What can I do for you, sir?" The man's suit was the most horrible shade of green he had ever seen, and there was a tone of arrogance to his voice that was extremely unappealing.

"I must speak with the artist... right away. The work in this gallery is outstanding."

"Well, thank you very much, sir, I appreciate your compliments. My name is Sam Barnett, and I'm the artist."

"You?" Jamison looked Sam up and down. "You were not what I was expecting. Are you sure it was you who painted all of these amazing pieces?"

"Yup. I'm positive. Is there something I can help you with?" Sam was trying his best to be polite and not get offended by this stranger, but his patience was wearing thin.

"Well..." Jamison pondered for a moment, looking at the paintings around him. "I suppose there is. My name is Jamison Shepherd." He took a dramatic bow and extended his hand to Sam who shook it hesitantly. "I am here from New York, and I will be the director of the next play at your town's theater. I am currently seeking an artist who can assist me in creating props and backgrounds that are realistic and of the highest standard. Your work stood out to me as I was walking past and I do believe that you have the talent that I need to create the perfect sets. Is this something that you would consider?"

Sam thought for a moment and then politely declined. "I appreciate the proposition, but I have a lot of work here at the shop. I can't afford to shut down every day to help out at the theater."

"Ah, but I don't think you understand," Jamison went on to explain. "Not only will I make it well worth your while financially," he leaned over and whispered a figure in Sam's ear, "but I also have connections in New York that could make you famous across the country and maybe even throughout the world."

Sam had been convinced. It wasn't necessarily the fame that he was after, but the figure that Jamison had whispered to him was more than six months' worth of sales from his shop. It was a no-brainer. He certainly couldn't refuse an offer like that. Extending his hand, he grasped Jamison's in his.

"You have yourself a deal, sir. I look forward to working with you."

"Excellent!" Jamison exclaimed. "You won't regret it!" And he turned with a flourish and left the shop.

CHAPTER THREE

After a long and busy day at the bakery, Melody left work and noticed that the whole town was buzzing. Both Melody and Smudge could sense that there was excitement in the air, it was almost electric. Stopping at the Koffee Korner for a quick coffee-to-go, Melody spied groups of people chatting and giggling. The normally mellow vibe of the cafe was much more energetic today. Unable to hold back her curiosity any longer, she made her way over to one of the groups.

"Hey, Melody!" One of the ladies called out a greeting. It was Eleanor Kincaid. Melody and Eleanor had had their differences in the past. Eleanor was a hard woman who would do anything to get what she wanted. But all of that had been put behind them, and they were quite friendly with each other now.

"Hello, Eleanor," Melody replied, smiling. "What's all the buzz about? I couldn't help but notice that something exciting seems to be going on! I don't want to miss out!" Smudge wagged her tail in agreement and perked up her ears, waiting to hear what the other lady had to announce.

"Oh, Melody! I can't believe you haven't heard the news yet! A big-time director, named Jamison Shepherd, from New York City, is in town! He's going to be putting on a production at our very own playhouse, and he's looking for actors and actresses for his play. I'm definitely going to audition, I was in the drama club in high school, you know." Then, leaning in closer she whispered, "Who knows, he may even make one of us a star!"

Melody smiled and nodded. "That is very exciting news, Eleanor! I'm sure you're guaranteed a part." Melody knew that Eleanor had had her fair share of drama in her personal life. It seemed plausible that she would be able to use her life experience to help her out on the stage!

"Plus, did you hear about Sam Barnett?" Eleanor continued.

Melody shook her head.

"It seems that Sam's art gallery really stood out to Mr. Shepherd when he arrived in town. He couldn't help but recognize Sam's amazing talent, and he's commissioned him to design the sets for the play! It's almost too much to take in! Imagine, all of this taking place in little ol' Port Warren." Eleanor shook her head in disbelief.

Laughing, Melody ordered her coffee and waved her goodbyes to the ladies. "Who would have thought that one man could get an entire town this worked up?" she asked Smudge as they continued home.

Smudge answered back with a yip and a wag of her tail.

Alvin was waiting for her when she arrived home, and he greeted her with a warm hug. She had been dating the town sheriff for some time now, and though they had been through a few hiccups and their fair share of adventures, things were going fabulously well. "Hello there, handsome!" she greeted him, and Smudge wagged her tail, saying hello as well. "How was your day?"

"Actually, things were pretty quiet today. I've been at the station, sitting at my desk for the most of it. Other than a few routine traffic stops, the town seems to be behaving itself. I have a feeling that everyone is too wound up about the appearance of this big-time producer to get into much trouble."

"So, you've heard about him too, have you? It seems as though this Jamison Shepherd character has really got a hold on this town. It's all anyone is talking about. Can you believe that Leslie spent a romantic evening with him last night... and was over three hours late for work this morning? I think I'll be happier when this play is over with, and everything goes back to normal around here."

Barking, Smudge agreed with Melody's sentiments, or maybe she just wanted her supper.

"Speaking of romantic evenings," Alvin chimed in. "I believe we have a double date tonight with Kerry and Bradford. You'd better go get changed, so we aren't late for our reservations."

Melody had almost forgotten about the dinner date.

Her mind had been filled with thoughts of the newcomer in town and his fancy New York style production. "Oh, heck, Al! I forgot all about dinner! Can you feed Smudge for me?" she called, and seeing him nod a yes, she took off running upstairs. It wouldn't take her too long to get changed out of her work clothes and into something a little more appropriate for a night out on the town.

Kerry and Bradford had chosen a delightful little restaurant, located right on the waterfront. A cozy patio offered a perfect view of the boats coming and going from the port. The weather was finally perfect for sitting out, and the sunset was absolutely gorgeous, casting romantic red and orange streaks across the sky.

Kerry and Bradford hadn't been dating long. It had been a difficult start for them, but things had been going well for a while now. They had all agreed that it was about time that the two couples spent an evening getting to know one another. When Bradford arrived in town, he had been carrying a lot of baggage and quite a few unsavory rumors following him around. It seemed that he had left his past behind him and was taking excellent care of Kerry so far.

Walking onto the restaurant's patio, Melody and Alvin spotted the other couple immediately. Joining them, they sat down and ordered drinks from the waiter who had followed them back there.

After the initial greetings, a long and uncomfortable silence drifted over the table. No one knew what to say or what topic to turn the conversation to. Kerry tried a few times, searching to find common ground between the two men, but her attempts were unsuccessful.

"Well," Melody cleared her throat uncomfortably. "Dinner is absolutely lovely. Thank you so much for inviting us." She kicked Alvin under the table and startled him into a coughing fit.

"Yes. Right. Absolutely lovely," he agreed, glaring at Melody while wiping his mouth with his napkin.

"At least it's nice and quiet here, unlike the rest of the town right now. Everyone is in such a buzz about that Jamison Shepherd and his new production, especially Leslie!"

"Did you say, Jamison Shepherd?" Bradford exclaimed, causing the whole table to jump. It was practically the first words he had spoken all evening.

Nods and mumbled affirmatives went around the table.

"Oh," Bradford said. "I've heard plenty of rumors about that man and trust me, none of them are good. I can't believe he's here in town."

"Really?" Alvin rested his arms on the table and leaned in towards Bradford, waiting for more information. When nothing came, he gave the man another prompt. "What type of rumors are we talking about here?"

"Let's just say it seems as though he has had his fair share of actresses fall under his spell. It seems he makes lots of promises, but then uses them and discards them for the next one."

Melody cast a worried look at Kerry. "I hope Leslie isn't in over her head." She let out a concerned sigh. And then, thinking to herself, tried to figure out if there may be a way to talk Leslie out of auditioning for the play. She thought it might be best to attempt to keep her away from Jamison, considering the hearsay about his sordid past.

Just then, the conversation was interrupted by an excited Leslie who burst out onto the patio, interrupting their gossip session and grinning from ear to ear.

"You guys will never guess what just happened!" Her hands were clasped in front of her chest." Guess who's going to be the leading lady in Jamison's new play?"

CHAPTER FOUR

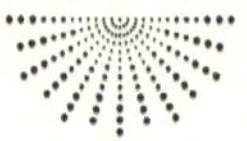

It didn't take long for the buds to begin to pop out on the trees and the first tulips of the season to bloom up from the ground. As the warmer weather of spring continued to creep into Port Warren, the excitement that Jamison's play had created, continued to grow. Many of the townsfolk were involved in the production now, and everyone was eager to see the final results of all of the hard work that was being put into the play. There was even talk that Port Warren could become the new Broadway, with a little help and influence from the new director.

Most of Leslie's spare time was spent down at the

theater rehearsing her lines and practicing her part. Kerry and Melody had to agree that she seemed to be the happiest she had ever been. Acting was definitely something she was passionate about, and she was putting her all into it.

One glorious Saturday, a few weeks after Jamison's arrival, Melody and Smudge headed downtown to open up the bakery. She wanted to try out a new recipe for a gluten-free, flourless version of her famous German chocolate cake.

"I think that this one is going to be a big success, Smudge!" she said.

Smudge, who had been fast asleep, let out a sigh at having been woken up.

"Everyone in town is so health conscious and looking for healthier versions of their favorite treats. It's important that Decadently Delicious keeps up with the times and offer them the alternatives that they want, don't you think?" Melody looked down to get Smudges input and realized that the pup was already fast asleep again, and was paying no attention to her ramblings. "Well then, I guess I'll take that as a hint."

Melody laughed, wiping her hands on a dishcloth, and sliding the tray of cakes into the oven to bake. "I feel as though, I shouldn't have to be talking to a dog anyways," she thought to herself. "Shouldn't I have an assistant here with me?" She checked her watch, and sure enough it was a quarter past eight. Leslie was late, again.

Heading up the hallway to the front of the shop, she stood at the large windows that faced onto the sidewalk and looked up and down the busy street. Peering this way and that she scanned for any sign of the girl who was supposed to have been at work fifteen minutes ago. Then, sure enough, off in the distance, a tiny figure could be spotted running towards the shop. The figure grew bigger by the second, and only a minute later, Leslie burst through the door, panting and out of breath, once again.

"Geez, Mel. I'm so sorry. I thought for sure I was going to make it on time. I ran the whole way here."

"Leslie, we've talked about this. I need you here, on time. You can't keep letting all of your extracurricular activities get in the way of your work priorities. This bakery needs you."

"I know, I know." Leslie was leaning up against the inside of the door, looking disheveled and still trying to catch her breath. "I had an early morning costume fitting down at the theater. I figured I would have tons of time to make it here. I was wrong. I'm really sorry. But I do have some exciting news!"

Melody waited in anticipation. It was hard to stay mad at someone who was always so enthusiastic and full of life.

"Jamison was speaking to me this morning and mentioned that there is one final role that needs to be filled for the play! He needs a dog, and I thought Smudge would be the perfect fit!"

Smudge's head lifted, and her ears pricked up at the mention of her name.

"Oh, no, Les. Thanks for thinking of us but we have lots of work to do here at the bakery, I don't have time to be running her off to practices and performances."

Smudge had sat up and seemed to be considering the prospect.

"I could take care of all of that for you, Mel. You wouldn't have to do a thing. I could pick her up and take her to practices and have her back here as soon as we were finished. She's the smartest and most well-behaved dog that I know. There isn't another dog in town who could play the role as well as she could! Please, Mel, she will be absolutely perfect for it!"

Smudge had trotted over and was now sitting beside Leslie. The French Bulldog was looking pleadingly at Melody with her head tilted in anticipation as if waiting for a response.

Melody laughed, looking at the pair, and took a moment to think it over. *It may not be such a bad idea,* she thought to herself. *I definitely don't need one of my friends falling under Jamison's spell, but having Smudge involved will allow me the opportunity to get an inside look at what's going on down at the theater. Maybe find out more about this Jamison Shepherd character and figure out exactly what his intentions are with Leslie.*

"Ok, fine." Melody declared. "Looks like you're going to be a star, Smudge!"

And with that announcement, Smudge let out a loud, excited bark and began wagging her tail excitedly.

"She's going to do great, Mel! Trust me, you won't regret it!"

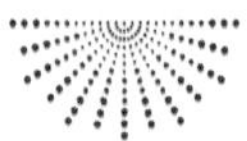

CHAPTER FIVE

The next day was Smudge's big rehearsal day, and Melody had decided to take her down to the theater herself and take a look around. The building was made of old brick and stone and stood at the west end of Front Street. There was a grand marquis over the entrance that was currently awaiting signage to announce Jamison's production.

The inside was just as old and luxurious as the outside. Plush carpets lined the front entrance, and all of the seats inside the theater were a deep, rich burgundy color, perfectly matching the heavy velvet curtains that hung on the stage.

Making their way down the steps between the rows and rows of seating, they headed towards the figures on stage, with Smudge excitedly in the lead. One man stood out from all of the others and seemed to be in control of the entire affair. Shouting out directions and commands and causing people to run frantically here and there in order to fulfill them. He wore a black pin-striped suit, and his dark hair was slicked back with what Melody assumed must have been an entire container of hair gel.

"That must be Jamison Shepherd, Smudge. He seems like a real peach." Melody looked down at the dog, who seemed hesitant about approaching now. "I'm sure it's just a busy day for him, girl. Don't worry."

Smudge wagged her tail with apprehension but continued towards the man, whose shouting was getting louder as they approached.

"No, no, no! I said stage left, not stage right! Come on people, pay attention here!" The yelling man threw his head into his hands in a dramatic display of disgust.

As Melody slowly approached him, she spied an elegantly dressed woman, hiding in the shadows, just off to the side of the stage. Her blond hair was perfectly set, and her clothes looked like they were purchased from a high-end designer store. She definitely wasn't one of Port Warren's residents, she looked far too glamorous to be from around here.

"Why in the world is there a dog in here?!" Jamison had finally spotted Melody and Smudge approaching. "Who on earth would you bring a dog into my production?!" He threw his arms up into the air in exasperation.

Melody wasn't about to be intimidated by this arrogant man. "My name is Melody Marshall, and this is my dog, Smudge. I was asked to bring her here today by your friend, Leslie Mathers, to audition for a role in your play." Melody could see the glamorous woman approaching, out of the corner of her eye. Jamison put his hand up to stop her.

"Oh, yes, why of course. I completely forgot that Leslie asked you to come here today. How silly of me. So, this is the dog that she was speaking of. Hmmm…" He crouched down onto the floor and inspected Smudge as if looking through the lens of a camera. "Mmmhmm," he murmured. "I think she just might do. She has the look I need, but does she have the skill? Let's see what this dog can do."

Smudge looked up at Melody quizzically, and Mel shook her head and shrugged her shoulders.

"Let's just see if this dog has it in her. I need her to catch a very important, incriminating letter when it is tossed through an open window." He gestured a throw flamboyantly with his arms as he explained. "The dog will jump, catch the envelope mid-air and then run off stage with it in her mouth where she will need to wait until the climax of the play when she will bring it back out. Think she can handle it?"

Before Melody could answer, Smudge barked confidently and ran up on stage, waiting to wow the audience with her acting skills. Melody turned to Jamison and laughed. "I think she'll be able to handle it just fine!"

Melody took a seat in one of the front row chairs and waited for the audition to start. Leslie appeared on stage and to Melody's delight, began acting out the scene. *She has got some amazing talent,* Melody thought, impressed at her friend's unexpected abilities. She said her lines perfectly and, exactly when cued, Smudge appeared on stage, leaped into the air, and caught the thrown envelope just as she should have. It was an absolute success, and Melody jumped to her feet to give the pair a standing ovation.

Jamison knew perfection when he saw it as well. "Well, Dog! You've got the job, I hope you don't mess it up on the big night."

Melody spoke up loud enough so Jamison could hear her. "Her name is Smudge, and I promise you she will be fabulous!"

Smudge jumped off the stage into Melody's arms, slathering her face with wet kisses. She was so proud of herself for doing such a great job and was excited to be a star. The wiggling of her little tail was proof enough of how she was feeling.

"It looks like she's pretty excited!" Leslie exclaimed to Melody, motioning towards Smudge.

"She did such a great job, Les, and so did you! I'm really impressed with both of you!"

"Thanks, Mel! And thanks for bringing Smudge down for the audition, I know that Jamison is really pleased with her. I promise you that I will bring Smudge to all of the auditions and take care of everything. You won't have to worry about a thing, except for making it here for the big premiere on opening night!" Melody thanked her friend and gave her a hug goodbye.

"I'll see you tomorrow at the bakery, bright and early... I promise I won't be late!" with that, Leslie ran off, and Melody clipped the leash to Smudge's collar, preparing to leave. She looked back one last time to wave goodbye but found that Leslie was already busy. She and Jamison had snuck off to the back of the theater and could now be found locked in each other's arms, sneaking a kiss.

Melody wasn't the only one who saw, though. Still in the shadows, the mysterious and glamorous woman from earlier was watching intently and looked none too pleased by the display.

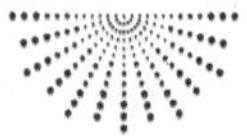

CHAPTER SIX

Touching up her makeup and running a brush one last time through her hair, Leslie was finally ready for her date with Jamison. She had picked out the perfect dress and had been practicing her lines on every break at work. Wanting to get perfection, hoping to impress him. Jamison hadn't been in town long, but they had been getting along fabulously and had been spending time alone together almost every day. Although he wasn't what she would consider her typical 'type,' Leslie had fallen head-over-heels for this strange character, and all of his oddities and unique ways were causing her to fall further under his spell.

Since she had to work late at the bakery to finish up

some big orders, the couple had agreed to meet at the restaurant for dinner. When Leslie arrived, the sight of Jamison's red convertible out front let her know that he was already inside waiting for her. He wasn't hard to spot when she entered, she could see him from the doorway. His red slacks and white shoes were not the usual dress for most of Port Warren's residents. Waving, she hurried over to the bar where he was seated, chatting away to the young bartender.

"Oh, hello there, darling," he said, rising to his feet and kissing both of Leslie's blushing cheeks. "How are you this evening?"

"I'm much better now, I must admit," she replied rather demurely. She wasn't sure why, but this man, made her feel shy. Perhaps it was his experience or the fact that he came from the city, but she felt like a young girl beside him. "I've been practicing my lines, you know," she boasted. "I think I almost have them all memorized now."

"That's very impressive, I must say." Jamison nodded in approval and bringing her tiny hand to his lips, kissed it. "There are a lot of things about you that impress me, my dear. Your amazing acting skills are just one of them." He peppered her hand with more kisses, causing Leslie to giggle with delight.

"I'm very glad to hear that." She smiled, "But seriously, Jamison, I want to find out how you really think I'm doing. I'm taking this acting thing very seriously, and I truly want to succeed at it. I feel like I could really go somewhere with all of this. I want your honest opinion, your true feedback. Please." Leslie looked at him pleadingly.

Jamison sat up in his chair. "All right, my love, let's talk business. Succeeding with this play is very important for me. I have the chance to really make a name for myself and to become one of the top directors in all of Manhattan. I would never, under any circumstances, cast someone, least of all my leading lady, who was not up to my extremely high standards. It is in my best interest to make sure that everyone who performs in any of my plays, does an outstanding acting job. I need people who know their lines, hit their marks, and are believable and passionate actors. You, my sweet Leslie, have all of this and more."

Leslie was smiling from ear to ear from all of his compliments.

"Leslie, you are truly an amazing actress who could really become something. Keep up the great work, and I'm sure that one day you will be a star!"

With her head full of thoughts of becoming famous and her heart overflowing with feelings for the man that sat beside her, Leslie enjoyed the rest of her evening with Jamison and silently dreamt of all that her future could hold.

CHAPTER SEVEN

Opening the door to the Koffee Korner, Melody was hit with the lovely aroma of freshly brewed coffee beans. The place was busy for a Thursday morning, and the pleasant sound of jazz music, combined with the chit chat taking place around the room, made for a warm and welcoming atmosphere.

Bradford sat at one of the corner tables, away from the rest of the crowd, and waved Melody over once she had finished placing her order.

"Thank you so much for taking the time to meet with me, Bradford," she said as she pulled out the chair across from him and sat down. "I was hoping that you could give me some more information on this producer fellow and fill me in on exactly what you have heard about his past? I'm a bit concerned that Leslie may be in over her head with him. Have you ever heard of him taking advantage of young actresses before?"

"As far as I know, Mel, that's all that Jamison does. From what I have heard, he has a history of taking in young ladies and getting their hopes up that they have a chance at stardom while he woos them. It has happened time and time again, with all of the productions that he has been a part of. Unfortunately, none of these ladies ever seem to make it to the stage. You see, Jamison Shepherd is involved in a long-time on-again, off-again relationship with the famous stage actress, Nicola Wilder. Nicola is rumored to be the one who gave Jamison his first big break and helped him make a name for himself in Manhattan. This happened years ago, and she still, to this day, uses this fact against him as a way to draw him back in under her wing whenever he starts to stray. In a way, you could say it's almost blackmail. If he looks like he's getting too comfortable with a new girl, Nicola swoops in and reminds him to whom he owes all of his success."

"Poor Leslie. I don't think she stands a chance with this guy." Melody shook her head in dismay.

Pulling out his phone, Bradford punched in a few characters, doing a quick search before he flipped it around for Melody to see. "You can see why the guy is always getting drawn back to her, I mean, for an older lady, she's absolutely stunning. It's still no excuse for what he does to all the other women who come into his life, though."

"Is that Nicola Wilder?" Melody asked, looking up at Bradford, a feeling of concern growing in the pit of her stomach. Bradford nodded as Melody continued. "I was down at the theater the other day, taking Smudge in for her audition, and this woman was there. She hid back in the shadows, just off stage, and watched every move that Jamison made. I'm certain it was her, though. She was dressed to perfection and had the air of a star about her. She only had eyes for Jamison and looked nowhere but in his direction. It seemed all very strange at the time, but it's starting to make sense now."

Bradford shook his head in disgust. "Sounds like the typical Jamison Shepherd scenario to me. This guy seems like he's a real creep."

"I agree with you, Brad, and I'm starting not to feel so good about this whole situation. I've got to get down to theater right now and talk to Leslie. I don't want to see her get her heart broken, and with Jamison's track record, I think it's inevitable if we don't do something quick." Gathering up her belongings and throwing her purse over her arm, it was only seconds before she was running out the door. "Thanks, Bradford!" she called over her shoulder and headed off towards the theater at a steady pace.

It didn't take her long to reach her destination, and walking inside, she found that rehearsal was underway and in full swing. Leslie was on stage with Smudge, who like the good pup she was, hit her mark perfectly again. Melody decided that speaking to Leslie now may not be the best course of action. It would be best to wait until she was alone and could focus on everything that Melody had to tell her. She took a seat in the back row and waited for rehearsal to end.

After running the actors through a few more scenes, Jamison stood up and announced that it was time for a meeting and an update on the play's progress. He called for the cast and crew to make their way to the front of the stage, where they all took a seat, watching Jamison intently for direction. He started off the meeting by giving praise to Sam Barnett for his outstanding artistic work on the set design, which Melody noted, was coming together quite nicely. Jamison continued by offering praise to Eleanor Kincaid. He stated that she was doing a magnificent job, and hers was an award-winning performance for a supporting role. It also appeared that Jamison had taken note of all of the hard work that Smudge had put into the production and offered his praise at the good job that she was doing as well. Melody smiled at this as she watched Smudge wag her tail. Then Jamison turned all of his attention to Leslie.

"Leslie, I'm sorry to have to say this," Jamison spoke loudly for all to hear but kept his eyes averted to the ground. "I just don't think you have it in you." He shook his head but still refused to look the girl in the eyes. "You're not hitting your marks, your lines are off, and honestly, you just don't have the experience that I need for a production of this caliber."

Melody couldn't believe what she was hearing. Leslie had been doing a fantastic job, and even an amateur like Melody could recognize that.

It was obvious that the words that Jamison had spoken cut through Leslie like a knife. Her eyes began to well up with tears, and her lip began to quiver. It took all of her self-restraint to keep from crying right there in front of everyone. Taking a deep breath to steady herself she spoke. "Jamison, I promise you, this play means everything to me. I will do better. I will practice harder, and I will be the best leading lady that you have ever cast." She tried to force a smile but Jamison's next words dashed any hope that was left in her.

"No, Leslie. I don't think you understand. There isn't enough time left for you to improve to the level that I need you to. I've already invested more than enough time trying to get you to where you need to be for this production, but it's too late now. I can't afford any more time."

No sooner were his words spoken than Nicola Wilder appeared from the shadows of the stage.

"Perhaps I can offer you a solution to your little problem, Mr. Shephard?"

"Ms. Wilder. What impeccable timing!" Jamison

declared. "I do believe you are just the solution I need. Everyone, this is Nicola Wilder, one of the greatest actresses to ever grace the stages of New York. Effective immediately, she will now play the leading role in this production. Perhaps you can all take some notes from an expert such as herself."

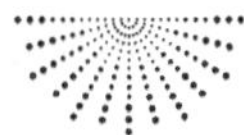

CHAPTER EIGHT

"Wait! Please, Jamison. Just give me a minute to speak to you in private. I'm sure we can work this through," Leslie shouted.

Jamison was hearing none of it. He had already turned his back to Leslie and was walking away.

"Perhaps you didn't hear him, but he said he didn't have any more time to waste with you," Nicola spat her words out vehemently, before following Jamison as he walked away. "I think it's about time that you collected your things and left," she called out over her shoulder with a smirk.

Melody couldn't believe the scene that was

unfolding before her eyes. *Poor Leslie* was all she could think. Springing to her feet, she rushed down the theater steps all the way to the stage and gathered her broken friend into her arms. "Oh, Leslie. It's going to be ok. I promise." Leslie let out a quiet sob into Melody's shoulder.

"This is absolutely ridiculous!" Sam Barnett, the stage set artist stood up and crossed his arms. "This is a local production, and the main part should be played by one of our local ladies. If you're not going to respect this town and its people then I'm done." He called out after Jamison. He threw down a paint-splattered rag in a show of protest.

Smudge started barking and growling as well, proving that she shared the same sentiment, and poor Leslie continued to cry in Melody's arms.

"Well, I don't know about the rest of you, but I have put a lot of time and energy into this production," Eleanor Kincaid shouted out from the back. "I am not about to quit now just because someone else wasn't putting in the required effort and couldn't do the job up to the director's standards."

These words hit home with Leslie, and she

straightened up. Wiping the tears from her eyes and taking a deep breath and clearing her throat for attention, she turned to the rest of the group. "Eleanor is completely right, guys," she sighed. "Just because I wasn't up to par, it doesn't mean that the rest of you should have to pay the price. You have all worked so hard and are doing such a great job. I just know that the play will be a big success with Nicola Wilder as your new leading lady. Please, don't let my failure bring this entire production down. Keep doing a great job, and I will be here to cheer you all on, on opening night." Leslie hung her head feeling defeated and embarrassed and walked backstage with Melody and Smudge to gather up her things.

"Oh, Melody." Leslie shook her head. "I really thought that I was doing a great job. I spent all of my spare time practicing and was exactly on point at every rehearsal. Jamison was always praising me, he never let on that I wasn't up to his standards. In fact, he never had any negative comments for me whatsoever. I just don't understand."

Melody tried to say something, and then she saw the truth dawn in her friend's eyes.

"It's all that Nicola's fault. If it weren't for her

showing up here and butting in where she doesn't belong, then I would still be the leading lady. I'd still be a part of this play." Entering the dressing room, the two ladies began gathering up Leslie's belongings.

"Hey, Les, was there anything else going on between you and Jamison? I mean anything more than just a professional relationship?" Melody couldn't hold back her question any longer. Ever since she had seen the two kissing in the back of the theater, it had been at the forefront of her mind.

Leslie looked at Melody and sighed. "I thought there was more between us, but I guess I was wrong. Let's just say that we shared more than a few 'special moments' both before and after I got the part. Do you think he was just using me? I feel so stupid." She zipped up her duffle bag and slouched down on the chair at the vanity table, her head in her hands.

"No." Melody put a hand on her friend's shoulder to stop her. "None of this is your fault, Leslie. You have to believe that." Crouching down in front of her to maintain eye contact, Melody shared all of the information that she had found out from her conversation with Bradford. "Listen, this isn't the first time that this scumbag has done something like this. It seems that he regularly takes advantage of young women before being pulled back in by Nicola. None of this is your fault, and I think it's best if you just move on from here and put this whole ordeal behind you."

"I don't know, Mel. I mean... I really thought there was something between Jamison and me. I really believe that he saw me as his leading lady, both on the stage and off. He said so numerous times. Why would he make something like that up?"

"What's this I hear about you being a leading lady?" Nicola Wilder laughed, walking into the dressing room and into the pair's private conversation at the most inopportune moment. "You think you could actually be someone's leading lady? Let alone the leading lady on stage? Please! Stop wasting everyone's time. You are just an amateur, and you shouldn't even be allowed to watch a play, let alone be in one."

After going through everything that she had this past afternoon, Leslie's emotions were running high. Nicola's comments were the final straw for her. At this moment, her anger got the best of her, and she charged at the woman. Arms flying, teeth bared, Leslie went at her with all that she had.

"I will kill you for this," she screamed as she flew across the space between them.

Fortunately for everyone, Melody managed to grab her as she ran past, and with considerable effort, restrained her and prevented her from doing any harm. Smudge, who had been watching and listening with concern as all of the events unfolded, began to growl. It seemed that she didn't care for Nicola all that much either, and was considering joining Leslie in her attack.

"C'mon, Leslie. Let's go. Let's try to leave with a little bit of our dignity intact." Melody took the girl by the arm and started pulling her out of the room, leaving Nicola behind looking appalled. Leslie struggled only a moment longer and then gave in to her good senses. Attacking Nicola would be satisfying, but in the long run, it would accomplish nothing.

Smudge trotted along at their heels, but she wasn't quite ready to leave yet either. Stopping in the middle of the floor, she turned and glared at Nicola and without a second thought, squatted and relieved herself on the dressing room rug.

Melody gave the other woman a look of disgust and made no effort to clean up the mess that Smudge had made. Snapping her fingers for Smudge to follow, the trio left, feeling somewhat satisfied at the outcome of their unexpected encounter.

CHAPTER NINE

The entire theater was in chaos after Jamison's words were spoken to Leslie. No one could believe what they had heard. Leslie had been doing a great job as far as anyone could tell and deserved her role as the leading lady. Much more than some stranger who had just set foot on their stage for the first time that afternoon. Opening day was quickly approaching, and with only a few rehearsals left before the curtain was lifted for all of Port Warren to watch, it was hard to believe that a newcomer could step in and be up to par, with so little time left.

The only one who seemed unaffected by the whole affair was Eleanor Kincaid. In her mind, her past drama training had made her an expert, and she had always questioned everyone else's abilities except her own. Wanting to ensure that her skills were up to Jamison's standards and looking for further compliments to boost her ego, she set off backstage to look for him.

Knocking on his office door, she heard him call out and entered without a moment's hesitation.

"Hello, Jamison. I just wanted to come back here and let you know that I think you made a very wise decision today. Leslie is a nice girl, but in my professional opinion, I think she should stick to baking. Acting isn't for everyone, as you well know. It takes a certain kind of person to be able to get up in front of an audience and pour your heart and soul into a performance. I'm just pleased that you think I'm doing such a good job."

"Yes, yes." Jamison waved his hand distractedly at Eleanor. He was obviously distraught. "You're doing a fabulous job. Keep up the good work." Eleanor noticed that he hadn't really been paying much attention at all to what she had been saying. Jamison was reading a letter that sat in his lap, and it held most of his thought. She could see that he was scrutinizing it over and over.

Perturbed that the director wasn't focusing more of his attention on her, she cleared her throat. "What's that you're looking at? It looks like it must be an important document of some sort." She was fishing for information.

"Hmm?" He looked up at her. "Oh, this? It's nothing really. Just a letter."

"Well, Jamison, it must be more than 'just a letter.' You haven't looked away from it since I walked into the room."

Sighing, Jamison put the letter on his desk and folded it up. "It's a letter from a New York production company. They are offering me a deal that I can't refuse. It's what I've always dreamed of, the chance I've always been hoping for." His voice was low, and he hung his head as he spoke.

"Well, that sounds like fantastic news! Congratulations, Jamison! Perhaps when you're casting for it, you can keep me in mind?"

"Yes, of course, Eleanor," Jamison replied, sounding sad.

"But I don't understand why you look so upset. This is the chance of a lifetime, you should be absolutely glowing."

"Oh, Eleanor, you don't understand. I have some loose ends that I need to tie up, and accepting this offer comes at a price. A very high price."

Eleanor looked at the distraught man. "I'm sure no matter what the price, it will be worth it."

Jamison hung his head even further. It was obvious something was very wrong.

CHAPTER TEN

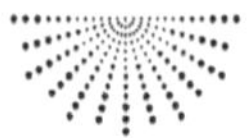

The drive through town to Leslie's house was a somber and quiet one. Although she didn't live far from the theater, everyone's mind was racing from the day's events, and it seemed to take forever to finally pull into her driveway. After seemingly hitting every red light along the way, the two girls, along with the faithful Smudge, had finally got her home.

"C'mon, Les. I think you should lay down and get some rest."

Leslie didn't move.

"It's been a stressful day, and a nice nap will be just the thing to clear your mind and calm your nerves.

Dealing with the likes of Nicola Wilder can sure take a lot out of a person."

Leslie nodded. She looked exhausted and worn down. She quickly agreed to Melody's suggestion.

Tucking Leslie into bed, Melody and Smudge sat with her until she fell asleep. When her gentle snoring started Melody turned to the pup, "Let's go, Smudge," she whispered. "She's off in dreamland now, and I think we should head down to the station and fill Alvin in on everything that's been going on."

Smudge quietly wagged her tail and gently hopped off the bed, careful not to wake their sleeping friend. The little dog followed Melody out of the house and back into the car.

The one place where Melody was always sure to find Alvin was at the Port Warren Police Department. Being the town sheriff definitely had its perks, especially when it came to getting free coffee and donuts. However, it was a busy job that kept Al occupied, even in his spare time.

Pulling up to the grey, stone building, Melody spotted Al standing outside, chatting to a few of his deputies. Waving, Melody and Smudge hopped out of the car and ran over to say hello.

"Hey, guys! What a nice surprise having you both show up and meet me at work like this!" Alvin was pleased to see them and gave Melody a big hug in greeting. Smudge wagged her tail excitedly and yipped at the sheriff, asking him for some attention too. "Don't worry, Smudge, I haven't forgotten about you!"

Bending over, he gave the pup a good rub and reached into his pocket to find one of the treats that he always kept there.

"Alvin, you will never believe the day that we have had," Melody started. She just couldn't hold back any longer. "It was just awful, and I feel so terrible for Leslie. That Jamison Shepherd is an appalling man and his partner, Nicola Wilder, is no better."

Alvin could see that Melody was distraught, and he put an arm around her shoulders to comfort her. "What happened, Mel? Tell me all of the details, starting right at the very beginning."

Melody took a deep breath and then recounted the afternoon's events for the sheriff from start to finish. "His treatment of her was so revolting, Al. Poor Leslie has been pouring her heart and soul into this production, and he has the nerve to tell her she's no good… right in front of everyone! The entire cast and crew! Leslie was mortified, as anyone would have been. And then, having that arrogant Nicola Wilder swoop in and take over like she owned the place! It was just too much. She said some really hurtful things to Leslie. It took all of my strength to hold her back. I think if I hadn't, Leslie might have given her a good wallop. Part of me thinks I should have let her."

Smudge yipped in agreement.

"Hearing all of the rumors that Bradford shared with us, I knew that Jamison didn't seem like the nicest guy, but I never expected him to be this bad. Leslie must be heartbroken right now. I'm going to head down to the theater and see if I can't "find" some kind of health code violation. I'll shut the whole operation down. That will teach Mr. Shepherd to mess with one of our friends. I'll have him packing his bags and wishing that he never set foot in Port Warren. That'll teach him." Alvin was beginning to get worked up. Hearing of all the wrongdoings that had just taken place was starting to make his blood boil.

"I don't think that's the answer, Al." Melody was trying to calm him down. "But I do hope that awful Nicola will get called back for a part in New York and leave Jamison high and dry. That would be a vindication."

"Is Smudge still going to be a part of the play?" Alvin looked at the pup, waiting for a response. She looked up at both Melody and Alvin and barked.

"I was planning on taking her out of the production all together but on second thought, keeping her in may be a good idea. It will give me the chance to see just what's going on at the theater. Plus, I'll be able to keep an eye on Jamison and make sure that he doesn't lead Leslie on again... or get into any other trouble for that matter."

Smudge wagged her tail, giving her consent.

"Actually, that sounds like a great idea. Why don't we head down there now and we can let Jamison know that he doesn't have to look for another dog. It will give me the chance to take a little look around." The sheriff was always looking for an investigation.

Taking Alvin's cruiser back down to the theatre, neither of them expected the scene that they were about to witness. The sheriff had barely put his car in park when they were both startled by a blood-curdling scream. Seconds later, Eleanor Kincaid, still in costume, came running out of the front doors.

"Oh, my god!" she screamed again.

"Eleanor, what's the matter? What's happened? Take a deep breath and tell us what's going on." Melody tried to calm the woman down, but it was no use.

"Nicola Wilder is dead!" The shriek that came out of Eleanor's mouth was deafening. "I just found her, lying dead in her dressing room. Oh, my god! Oh, my god! Oh, my god!"

Alvin's training kicked in as second nature, and he ran inside to quickly assess the situation. Melody and Smudge were only steps behind. They made their way past the stage and through the back hallways to the dressing room. Throwing open the door, they found Jamison, leaning over the actress's lifeless body.

Running to Nicola, Alvin pushed the director out of the way. Expertly feeling for a pulse, he shook his head gravely.

"Nothing. She's gone."

Grieving for only a moment, Alvin swiftly turned on Jamison. He pulled out his handcuffs. "Jamison Shepherd, you are under arrest. Anything that you say or do..."

"Wait! Sheriff! I swear to you. I am an innocent man. Nicola was one of my closest friends. I swear, I would never do anything to harm her, not in a million years! I came here to check on her. I wanted to see how she was making out, settling into her new dressing room. I came to see if she needed anything. When I walked in, I found her like this, just like Eleanor did."

Eleanor, who had managed to pull herself together slightly, had joined the group in the dressing room and took offense at Jamison's words. "What do you mean, Jamison? Bringing my name into it as though I had something to do with this terrible tragedy! I was simply walking by and saw her door open a crack. Wondering what a real star's dressing room would look like, I took a peek. This is the ghastly sight I saw!"

"Eleanor, please. I wasn't trying to accuse you of anything. I was simply stating the fact that I am no more guilty of this crime than you are. It was by chance that both of us stumbled upon this horrific scene." Jamison took an elaborate bow towards Eleanor, asking for her forgiveness. "Sheriff Hennessey, I challenge you to find proof of my involvement in this crime. Nicola was obviously pushed into her vanity, and I swear to you that my fingerprints will not be present on either the table or the mirror nor anything else for that matter."

Looking around, Alvin could see that Nicola had

been pushed into her mirror. It was broken, as were a number of the lights that framed the mirror. The rest were no longer lit and the way they framed the broken glass told a very different tale of stardom. The actress had been preening herself, preparing for her performance, but now the final curtain had been called.

The floor was scattered with broken glass, items of makeup, and the table that had collapsed under Nicola Wilder's weight. Alvin knew that he would have quite the job ahead of him trying to find any clues in the clutter, but luckily, he was always up for a challenge.

"Jamison, as sheriff of this town, that's my duty. If I don't find your fingerprints, then I will definitely find those of the person responsible for this crime." Though he said that he knew it was unlikely. The killer would have pushed her head, and that was one place they couldn't get fingerprints from. Maybe they could get DNA, but if it was Shepherd then his DNA could be on her anyway, as could anyone else's who was in the play.

Alvin bit back a sigh. This didn't look good for Leslie. She had a motive, she had shouted that she would kill the woman, and she knew the layout of the place well. After all, that was her dressing room just hours before. At least she was at home and well away from the crime scene. With that, he stepped aside and made a call to police headquarters to report the crime and call for back-up from his deputies and the coroner. It was time to investigate the scene.

Turning to Melody, Jamison wore a worried look on his face. "So, how is dear Leslie doing? She was rather upset the last time I saw her."

Melody looked the man over with a scowl. His concern didn't seem genuine. After all that she had heard about him, combined with the current situation that she had just found him in, she wasn't willing to trust him and give him the satisfaction of an answer, so she continued to stare.

"Look, I know you saw what went on here this afternoon out on stage, but I swear that I was truly developing real feelings for the girl. She was kind and sweet, and we had a lot in common, believe it or not. We were really starting to get along well. It's a difficult situation though. I'm only in town for a short time, and Nicola and I have worked together for so long. When she showed up here it brought back a lot of old feelings. She really has a pull on me. Plus, she is an amazing actress and could have added a lot of value to the production. You know how it is, right?"

Melody shook her head. She had no idea how someone could be so heartless. Watching Jamison, she thought she caught the faintest hint of a smile cross his lips.

"I saw Leslie back here this afternoon, you know. I walked past the door just as she lunged at Nicola. She seemed to be filled with rage. It's a good thing that you stopped her when you did, things could have gotten very ugly. Well actually, I suppose things did end up getting very ugly." He looked around the murder scene and put a finger up to his lips as he thought. Then he spoke slowly and deliberately. "I certainly hope Leslie didn't come back here to finish the job she started."

"Leslie would never!" Melody finally spoke, appalled at this man's accusation.

"No, no. Of course, she wouldn't! It was just a silly thought. I never should have spoken it aloud. I feel terribly guilty now." The look on his face didn't show any sign of the guilt that he spoke of.

Melody was sure that this man had never felt a moment of remorse in his life, and although she knew that Leslie wasn't capable of committing such a crime, she couldn't help but feel that she should head back and check on her. Just to make sure everything was ok. Turning her back on Jamison, Melody headed over to Alvin and told him of her plan.

"That's a good idea, Mel. I think its best if you and Smudge head back to Leslie's, make sure she is safe and fill her in on what's been going on around here. I'm going to start questioning the cast and crew and see what information they have to share, and the deputies should be here momentarily to start collecting evidence and dusting for prints."

"Leslie's prints will be all over the room, it was hers until..."

"I know," Alvin said. "Look, we both know Leslie didn't do this, but I may have to question her. A lot of people saw her reaction."

Melody nodded. "I will go see her."

Alvin smiled. She could see he wanted to hug her, but he had his sheriff's head on and knew it would be inappropriate. Instead, he reached down and squeezed her hand. It was a small gesture, one that no one could see, but it meant the world to her.

"Go," she said. "Go prove she's innocent."

Alvin nodded and walked off.

Melody sighed and looked around. It looked as though Alvin and the Port Warren Police Force would have a busy day ahead of them, so Melody gladly accepted this opportunity to sneak away and find out how Leslie was feeling.

Heading back to Leslie's house for the second time that day, Melody was making a chronographic list of all of the day's events in her head. She wanted to keep track of who said and did what and in what order. She knew that being organized and efficient was the best way to figure out who committed a crime and would make catching them, that much easier.

It didn't take her long to arrive at Leslie's place, but immediately after getting out of the car, she could sense that something was wrong. "Something feels different, eh Smudge?" She looked down at the little bulldog who barked back her agreement. The house was quiet and unusually dark. The pair made their way up the front steps and opened the front door. Stepping inside, the house seemed even more quiet than it looked from the outside and doing a quick sweep of the entire place, it quickly became clear that Leslie was nowhere to be found.

"This is really strange, Smudge. Where could Leslie have gone?"

Smudge lowered her front end down and covered her eyes with her paws. It was her latest trick, to take a bow, and it certainly summed up how Melody was feeling.

"I know, it's not like her to wander off like this, especially after the rough day that she has had." Smudge jumped up, spun around, and then sat, cocking her head to one side, as if to say that she too had no idea where the girl could have gone.

Pulling out her cell phone, Melody hit Leslie's

number on speed dial. The call went straight to voicemail. Melody shook her head, Leslie always had her phone on and picked up her calls right away. Calling back a second time, it went directly to voicemail again. This time she left a message, asking her friend to call her back as soon as she got the message.

Unsure of what to do next, but knowing that she needed to do something to try and find Leslie as quickly as possible, Melody called Kerry. She let out a sigh of relief when Kerry picked up on the second ring.

"Hey, Mel!" Kerry's cheery voice rang through the line. "How is everything?"

"Listen, Kerry," Melody's voice was straight to the point. "Something has happened down at the theater. Something terrible. I took Leslie home this afternoon and just came back to check on her, but she's missing. I need your help."

"Oh, my god!" Kerry's voice was filled with concern. "Bradford and I are on our way. Just hang tight, Mel, we will be there in a few minutes."

When Kerry and Bradford arrived, Melody filled them in on all of the day's events starting from Jamison's kicking Leslie out of the production and Leslie's near attack on Nicola, right down to the very end, where Nicola's body was found dead on her dressing room floor, just a short time ago.

"I feel like all of this is my fault," Melody berated herself. "I should never have left her alone today. I should have been there with her to comfort her while she slept and to talk to her when she woke up. In fact, I never should have allowed her to be a part of the play in the first place. I should have done everything in my power to try and stop her."

"Hey, listen, Mel," Kerry offered some consolation. "None of this is your fault, whatsoever. Your words would never have made a difference. Leslie was in love, and those feelings trump everything else, even rational thought! I know as much first hand." She smiled and looked over at Bradford, who returned her gaze with a wink. "She needed to see for herself how much of a cad Jamison was for her to believe that it wouldn't work out between them. Nothing that any of us could have said or done would have stopped her."

Melody knew her friend was right. Leslie had fallen head-over-heels for Jamison and was so star-struck by his production that no amount of convincing from anyone else would have changed her mind. But that didn't change the fact that Leslie needed them now. So where was she?

"Thanks," Melody said. Though logically, she already knew what Kerry had told her, it was nice to hear someone else say it.

"You don't think...?" Kerry asked.

"No, I don't," Melody said. "Maybe she was mad enough to hit her earlier, but even then, not hard enough to kill her. I think it's more likely that weasel, Jamison.

"I don't know," Bradford said. "From what I've heard, he would have too much to lose. She has backed him a lot in the past, and I think she still does."

"Well, maybe we should let the sheriff investigate, for once," Melody said with a smile. "Let's go find our friend."

They all nodded, and Smudge jumped up and down on the spot barking happily.

"I think it's best if we split up," Bradford said. "We can cover more ground that way. I'll head south towards Main Street and you girls, stick together, and head towards the Decadently Delicious. I'll loop around and meet you there, in say, a half an hour? And keep your phones on, just in case!"

"That sounds like the perfect plan, honey. Be safe, and I'll see you soon." Kerry leaned in for a kiss, and the two shared a private moment, looking into each other's eyes.

Smudge, with something of a smile on her face, looked up at Melody, and she laughed back at the dog. Watching the couple, though, the realization came to Melody that there was a lot more between them than what she had previously thought.

Waving goodbye to Bradford, the two girls headed up the street in the direction of the pastry shop. Smudge was sniffing the pavement and wanted to go in the other direction, she wanted to follow Bradford.

"No, girl, come with us, we have to find Leslie,"

Smudge gave a whine and a bark and then turned and ran in front of them, sniffing for clues, just ahead of them. "You and Bradford seem to be doing really well, Kerry."

"Oh, he is such a wonderful guy. I know that he came with a bit of a bad track record, but he is really proving to me that people can change for the better. I'm really in love with him." Her eyes took on a dreamy, faraway look as she spoke of him and Melody realized that things were pretty serious between the pair. Kerry was actually considering a future with this man. It made her happy that at least one of her friends had found true love. Maybe Jamison was able to change as well? Maybe there was still a chance for Leslie and him?

The girls had walked up and down the town, through the quaint little side streets and even down by the waterfront, but there was still no sign of Leslie. They had made their way to the bakery and Melody pulled out her keys, unlocked the door and let them inside. They had just sat down with tea and scones to discuss what to do next when the front door chimes rang. It was Bradford, and by his side was a distraught looking Leslie.

Both Kerry and Melody jumped to their feet and ran to the girl.

"Oh, sweetie, are you ok?" Melody now realized that Smudge had smelt which direction Leslie had gone. They should have let the little dog lead them right to her. She would remember in the future, and she leaned down and rubbed Smudge's head. "Sorry, girl," she whispered. Smudge sighed in delight at the love she was receiving.

"What happened to you? Where were you?"

"Well, I woke up and decided to go for a long walk to try and clear my head," Leslie explained. "I was fine, there's no need to worry. While I was walking, Bradford found me. He said that all of you were out looking for me. That's when he filled me in on what happened at the theater. What happened to Nicola. It's terrible. I mean, I just can't believe it." She shook her head solemnly.

Melody put her arm protectively around the girl's shoulder. "Don't worry, Leslie. I am going to do everything in my power to keep you safe until Alvin can get to the bottom of this case."

Smudge ran around Leslie's feet barking, proving that she would do the same.

Looking from one to the other, Leslie smiled. "Thanks, guys, I really appreciate it, but I don't think any of that is going to be necessary. I know who the murderer is. I've already solved the case."

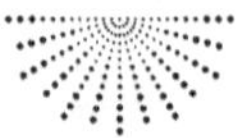

With the police investigation in full swing in the back of the theater, Jamison decided that it was best not to waste any more time. After all, the show must go on. He had gathered up all of the cast and crew for the second meeting that day. Everyone was in a buzz about what had happened and why the police were there. The rumors were flying.

"Settle down, please! Everyone! Quiet!" Jamison called out his orders, and eventually the stage became silent. All eyes were on him, waiting for an explanation.

"As some of you may already be aware, there has

been a horrific accident backstage today. Nicola Wilder was found dead in her dressing room."

There were gasps and whispers in response to this information.

"Now, there is no need to worry. It seems as though it was an isolated event, and the Port Warren Police Force has everything under control. They just ask for our cooperation. If anyone has any information or has witnessed anything at all, please let the deputies know. We all know that there were some hurt feelings this afternoon and some of us became a bit upset, just be sure that the sheriff is aware of everything that went on." With his speech complete and all of the formalities out of the way, Jamison was ready to get down to work.

"Now, as for the production, the play will still be taking place. Since we currently lack a leading lady, I would like to promote Eleanor to the starring role. So far, she has been putting in a lot of hard work, and I think she can handle the demands that this part requires."

Eleanor nodded her agreement and smiled broadly. She was absolutely thrilled. Her high-school drama days were definitely paying off now, and a chance at being on the stage in the Big Apple may actually become a reality.

"Jamison!" The man turned at hearing his name called from the back of the theater. It was Melody and her dog, and they were making their way down to the front of the stage.

"Smudge is here, Jamison. We talked it over and gave it some thought and decided that despite all that has happened, Smudge should still be in the play. We made a commitment to both you and the whole production, and we would like to honor it."

"Oh, well, that's a pleasant surprise! After our conversation earlier, I wasn't expecting to see either of you again. This is fantastic news!" He clapped his hands together. "Thank you, Melody, the last thing I need right now is another pesky complication right before opening night!"

A few days passed and practice went on as usual, as did Alvin's investigation into the suspicious death of Nicola Wilder. Jamison had been to him and asked if Leslie was being charged. Alvin had to tell him that although she had a motive there was no evidence to prove she committed the crime.

"Then perhaps it was Eleanor Kincaid," Jamison said. "After all, she now has the leading role in the play. That is surely a motive for murder!"

Alvin had smiled politely and said that he would look into it. Eleanor was certainly a pushy woman, but she didn't know she would get the part before the murder... did she? Alvin didn't know, and so he decided to ask around. This was one difficult case, for there seemed to be no evidence. Surely, the murderer would have some blood splatter on their clothes. All he had to do was work out who's room to search.

The evening of the show's opening night was lovely and warm. It was the perfect evening for the people of Port Warren to be out and about, which most of them were. The theater was packed, with standing room only. It was a full house. Melody took Smudge backstage while Alvin waited in the audience. As she walked down the corridor, Smudge barked at one of the doors.

"What is it, girl?" Melody asked.

Just at that moment, Jamison came out of the room.

Melody scowled at the director and laughed a little. "I guess you heard him," she said to Smudge. "Hurry along, girl, I want to get back in the audience to watch the show.

Smudge barked and then trotted along with her.

Watching from the wings, Melody quickly became aware that Eleanor Kincaid was a terrible actress and was doing an awful job in the leading role. Unable to bear it any longer, she made her way backstage to Jamison. He stood, leaning against the wall for support with his head in his hands.

"She's horrible, isn't she?" he muttered as Melody approached.

"Well, she definitely isn't the best leading lady that you could have chosen," Melody agreed, not trying to hide her true feelings. "How are you going to be able to recover from such a disastrous show, Jamison? The media will have a field day with this one. It's certainly not your best performance."

Sighing, Jamison shook his head. "I have no idea. I guess I will have to return to the big city and start over from scratch. I don't see any other choice now. My reputation will be ruined. I have to admit, though," he looked up at Melody, "I really did have hopes that I could stay here with Leslie. We could run our own little production business. Start a family. It would have been wonderful."

Melody wasn't sure if the wistful look in Jamison's eye was legitimate or not, and she wasn't given the opportunity to ponder on it. Listening to the production going on onstage, she knew that Smudge's big debut was just moments away and not wanting to miss the pup's appearance, she excused herself and ran out to the theater to watch.

Eleanor began to read the letter that was to be thrown for Smudge to catch. As she got a few sentences in, she stopped acting and realized that it wasn't the prop letter that she was accustomed to practicing with. She looked around the audience and seeing no other option, continued reading.

"It is our great pleasure to announce that you, Jamison Shepherd, have been chosen as the lead director in our next big Broadway production in Manhattan. I'm sure that you will agree that this is the opportunity of a lifetime, and it is yours for the taking, as long as you don't bring with you any of the "complications" that we spoke of before." Eleanor stopped reading and looked up, bewildered.

Jamison, who had followed Melody up to the front of the house had frozen in his tracks and watched, with eyes wide, as Leslie took the stage.

"Good evening, ladies and gentlemen," she spoke with the flair of an actress. "I am here to inform you that Nicola Wilder was murdered backstage, in this very theater and the murderer stands in this very room with us now. Jamison Shepherd, the director of this play, is the one to blame for her ruthless killing. He knew that Nicola would never relinquish the hold that she had on him and therefore he would never be able to release her grasp. He had no hopes of advancing his career any further while she was still alive. She would never have allowed it. No big-time Manhattan playwright would be interested in a director who came with so much baggage. Jamison was intentionally cruel to me and dropped me as the leading role of this production so that he could get me riled up and angry with Nicola for taking over the lead. He proceeded to murder Nicola backstage but hoped that my anger and jealousy towards her would put all of the suspicions on me, leaving him free to finish up here before moving back to New York to direct the play of his dreams." Leslie took a bow.

"Liar!" Jamison cried out from the audience." I would never do such a thing, Nicola was my friend.
"

"Actually," Eleanor had stepped up from the background. "Just the other day, Jamison was telling me a similar story about being presented with a great opportunity and wishing that he could find a way to "tie up some loose ends." It was all very suspicious." She seemed pleased at being privy to this information.

Just at this moment Smudge trotted onto the stage with a shirt in her mouth. She trotted all the way across the stage, down the steps, and over to Melody. Melody took it from her.

"Look, it has blood on it," she said holding it out to Alvin. "Good girl." She stroked Smudge.

"That's not mine," Jamison said. "You can't prove it's mine, and that dog didn't have a search warrant."

At that there was a roar of laughter from the people in the audience.

Alvin stood up. "Face it, Shepherd, you've been caught." Then turning to address the rest of the audience, Alvin continued. "You see, folks, Jamison here was hedging his bets. He was hoping that by belittling Leslie in front of the rest of the cast, and by giving Nicola Wilder the new role of the leading lady, he would upset Leslie enough, and all suspicion would be directed towards her, instead of on him. We also found more evidence in Nicola's personal diary. It appears that she had feared for her safety and had wondered for some time when Jamison might try to harm her. At one point she even wrote, and I quote, *'I wonder when he is going to man up and murder me?'* "

Jamison, looked panicked and cried out his confession. "All right, all right! You've caught me!"

Alvin made his way over to the man who had dramatically flung himself to the floor. "Jamison, this time, you are officially under arrest." He continued to read him his rights as he snapped the handcuffs over his wrists and pulled him to his feet. The rest of the deputies who were waiting offstage came out to take over for the sheriff.

Melody had joined Leslie on stage and gave her a big hug. Without her putting all of the pieces together, they may never have caught Jamison. After hearing about Jamison's past and putting together all of the loose ends, she knew that he was to blame and came up with this elaborate way to force him to confess in front of the entire town.

Eleanor came over to join the ladies in a hug as well, and Melody thanked her for playing her part in revealing the director's plan perfectly.

The audience was blown away by all that they had seen and pleased at getting much more than what they had paid for. Everyone jumped to their feet with applause. As the thick, velvet curtains were slowly drawn to a close, Smudge looked around at the room full of people clapping and cheering. She proudly took center stage and wagging her tail, she took her bows and basked in the ovation that she was sure was being given just for her.

CHAPTER FOURTEEN

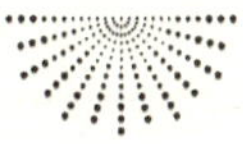

Spring was now in full bloom in Port Warren, and the whole town was in an uproar about the horrible murder at the theater. No one could believe that they had all been fooled by the production's director, Jamison Shepherd. He had done a good job at keeping his true character hidden, and it would be a long while before any of them trusted a big city director again. If the town thought that he caused a stir when he came to town, it was nothing compared to the frenzy he created as he was leaving. Everyone who was anyone at all was talking about the story, long after Mr. Shepherd was arrested and charged with the violent murder of Nicola Wilder. He was sentenced to a lifetime term in a New York prison, and all of the townsfolk were pleased that he would never be able to disrupt their peaceful seaside town again. It appeared that the only stage that Jamison would appear on anytime soon would be at the state courthouse when he took the stand to plead his defense.

No one was quite as happy with this news, however, as Leslie, who felt that luck was on her side with this whole ordeal. The fact that it could have been her lying dead on a dressing room floor was one that she would never forget.

Down at Decadently Delicious, things had gotten back to normal. With Easter well on its way, the girls at the bakery were filling the shelves with pastel-colored cakes and cookies. Everything was brightly decorated for the season, and baskets of freshly dyed Easter eggs were elegantly placed throughout the store.

Melody and Leslie were in the back kitchen, trying out a new vegan recipe for carrot cake that was sure to be a best-seller when they were interrupted by the ring of the front door chimes.

"Hello?" A deep voice called out from the front of the store.

Melody wiped her hands on a tea towel and threw it over her shoulder as she walked out of the back and up to the front counter, Leslie following along behind her. "Well, hello there!" she greeted the artist, Sam Barnett and his beautiful, blonde girlfriend, Claudia Conway, who was at his side. "You must be here to pick up some desserts for Easter dinner?" Melody assumed.

"I could never say no to any of your delicacies, Melody! But the real reason for our visit today is to talk to Leslie."

Surprised, Leslie turned her full attention to Sam.

"Although the previous production down at the theater didn't go exactly to plan, I still really enjoyed most of the time that I spent there. Developing the sets was a new and exciting way for me to express my creativity, and I spent a lot of time talking to Jamison and learning the ropes on how to put together a play. I've given it a lot of thought, and I think I'm ready to direct my own production."

"That's fantastic news, Sam!" Melody was happy that Sam had found a new calling.

"And in my first production, I want Leslie to play the

leading role. You proved to all of us how amazing of an actress you are, and I think you will be absolutely perfect for my play. You will fit the role of the leading lady quite well. I'm really hoping that you'll consider it?"

"Wow, Sam," Leslie was speechless. "I really don't know what to say. I'm so honored that you would consider me for the part, but I think I will have to decline. After all that went on with Jamison's production, I think it's best if I spend some time living in the real world for now and focus more on my job here at the bakery."

"Oh, Les! But you're such an amazing actress!" Melody was surprised that the girl hadn't jumped at the opportunity. Being on stage for her was like putting a fish in water, she was a natural. "I don't think you should completely close the stage door."

Turning back to Sam, Leslie promised that she would consider the proposition and get back to him, but that she wasn't making any hasty promises. Thanking him for his consideration, both girls said goodbye to the couple and got back to work.

"Mel?" Leslie turned to her friend. "Thank you so

much for always being there for me and for looking out for me. I know that there are times when I should have paid more attention to your advice. If I had, then I may not have ended up in such a mess with that man."

"Aw, Les," Melody leaned over and gave Leslie a heartfelt hug. "You know that no matter what, I am always here for you girls. We're a family, and family looks out for each other." Barely finishing her sentence, Kerry unexpectedly popped into the kitchen.

"What's this I hear about family? Are you guys having a tender moment without me?!" The three girls laughed and joked, just like sisters.

"I wanted to stop by and see if you girls were free this evening to join Bradford and me for a special dinner. It's been ages since we have all been out together, and I thought it was about time, considering all of the recent events, that we took some time off to just relax and have a little fun!"

"That sounds like a great idea to me!" Melody said, and Leslie nodded in agreement.

"Perfect! We will see you around six."

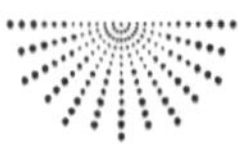

CHAPTER FIFTEEN

After meeting Alvin at her place, the pair had made their way downtown to a fancy, upscale restaurant located in Port Warren's finest hotel. Each table was elegantly set with white table cloths, and real silver cutlery and a beautiful, candle centerpiece glowed at each one. The ambiance was beautiful. The hostess led them to a secluded table in a private room, where Leslie, Kerry, and Bradford were already waiting for them. Once the waitress had served them their drinks, Bradford got to his feet.

"I just want to take a moment to propose a toast. Cheers to Sheriff Hennessy and Melody for doing such an amazing job at catching Jamison and putting a murderer behind bars. Cheers to Leslie for discovering her newfound acting talents and for playing her part in capturing a criminal. Finally, cheers to Kerry for putting up with me. I see a lot of similarities in the way that Jamison treated the women he dated and the way that I used to be. I'm not proud of that fact. But I've made a decision to change, and since I can't change the man that I was, I'm going to change the man that I'm turning into. Kerry, I promise you that I will do my very best to be the man that you have always wanted and the man that you need. I may not be perfect, but I want to be perfect for you."

Everyone's eyes were wide as they watched Bradford produce a ring box from his back pocket and get down on one knee. Even guests from the neighboring tables were beginning to listen in and stare.

"Kerry, you are the love of my life, and I want to be with you until the very end. Will you do me the honor of becoming my wife?"

Complete silence had fallen all around, even the waiters had paused to find out what her answer would be.

The surprise on Kerry's face was evident. She had

been expecting nothing more than a nice relaxing dinner with her friends. A marriage proposal was the last thing on her mind.

Her eyes were wide, and she was staring down at Bradford, trying to piece together exactly what was going on. All of a sudden it all seemed to sink in and her look of bewilderment changed to one of pure joy and excitement. "Yes!" she shouted and the entire restaurant erupted with whistles, shouts, and cheers of congratulations.

Bradford jumped to his feet, picked Kerry up in his arms and swung her around. The rest of the group was clapping and laughing. The unexpected proposal was just the thing to lighten the mood and lift everyone's spirits after all of the recent occurrences.

"Wait, everyone, please." Bradford raised his hand to silence the table. "I have one more surprise. Kerry, to celebrate our engagement, I've booked a tropical, all-inclusive beach vacation. I think it's time that we get away from some of this chaos and spend some one-on-one time. What do you say?"

"Oh, Bradford!" Kerry exclaimed. "I don't know what

to say. It's all just so much to take in at one time! Of course, I'll go. I'd absolutely love to! That is, if I can get the time off work?" Kerry turned to Melody questioningly.

Laughing, Melody nodded. "Of course, you can go! You deserve it. Go and have a wonderful time, but don't forget to take lots of pictures!"

Kerry gave Melody a big hug, thanking her profusely as she did, then she and Bradford got to work talking over their vacation plans and discussing wedding ideas, each one talking a mile a minute. The happiness that they each felt was evident in their voices and was written all over their faces.

Melody leaned over to Leslie, placing a hand on her arm. "They seem really great together, don't they?" Melody asked, and Leslie nodded. "Listen, Les, don't be downhearted. Your turn will come too, you've just got to give it some time to find the absolutely perfect guy. He's out there, I promise."

"I know, Mel. I haven't given up just yet. One day I know I'm going to be just as happy as you and this guy," she said, gesturing towards Alvin, who was standing with his hand outstretched to Melody.

"Dance with me?" he asked Melody, who smiled up at him.

"Go!" Leslie urged.

Arm in arm, the couple waltzed around the dancefloor. The evening had turned out even more perfect than Melody could have imagined. Things had finally settled down again in Port Warren and love was definitely in the air this spring.

As the sun began to set over the harbor, the group of friends talked and laughed and danced the night away, content in each other's company and happy that their lives were drama-free, once again, until their next adventure.

If you enjoyed this book then grab the first book in this much loved series Strawberries and Sweet Lies

SMUDGE AND THE STOLEN PUPPIES – PREVIEW

Smudge and the Stolen Puppies – Preview

"No one breathe!"

Melody Marshall, Port Warren's pride pastry chef, extended her steady hand toward the cake. It was special, one she planned on entering in the town's Annual Spring Bake-Off. "Don't move a muscle!" Melody whispered to anyone in earshot.

She had modeled the cake after the one thing that gave her the most joy in life – *and no, it wasn't Alvin Hennessey, her fiancé.* The cake was a three-dimensional layer cake, covered in buttercream strategically dyed a grey-blue, to resemble her sweet

French Bulldog, Smudge! Every detail up until this moment was done to perfection. She only needed to apply the finishing touch – a smudge on the cake's back to match the real one.

Behind Melody, her friends and recently promoted business partners of the Decadently Delicious bakery debated the pros and cons of a potential new addition to their group. This new addition was a puppy.

"I love dogs just as much as the next person," Leslie said. "I just don't understand why you won't wait a little bit longer. You have a new husband, more responsibility with the bakery ... a puppy is very demanding,"

"Because I want one now," Kerry Porter whined dramatically. "Bradford wants one, but when he gets back from his training ... and Melody wouldn't mind." She quickly glanced at Melody, who was laser-focused on the cake. "Would you, Mel? Smudge could use the company. Right, Smudge?"

Smudge sat just to the left of Melody's feet. She lifted her front paws and barked in agreement!

"Perhaps we can discuss this after I finish the cake?" Melody said. Her usually steady hand started shaking as she carefully applied a proper smudge-like section of frosting.

Kerry and Leslie paused their discussion and watched Melody work. Standing mere inches from her, each woman watched over Melody's shoulders. They held their breath with anticipation.

"Voilà!" Melody shouted excitedly, a heartbeat later.

The ladies exhaled a deep sigh of relief in unison, and Smudge hopped up onto her back legs. She spun in a circle of celebration! Melody raised her arms triumphantly. "I can't wait to show this cake off at the festival." She exclaimed proudly. Leslie and Kerry applauded her success.

"I'm expecting it to take home a blue ribbon, Mel." Kerry cheered. "I bet the paper will do a story on it since it looks just like her! The icing is the perfect shade of *Smudge.*"

"An article in the paper would draw a lot of attention to the bakery," Leslie said excitedly. Always an excellent business partner, she made a note of the potential opportunity to bring more attention to the bakery.

"Indeed, it would." Melody nodded as she removed her chef's jacket. Creating this cake had been a personal challenge for Melody, and now she was both relieved and proud of her accomplishment. "C'mon, Smudge, let's get some fresh air before the day gets crazy. We've got dinner with Alvin tonight." She attached Smudge's leash to her collar.

Together, they stepped out of the bakery into the warm spring air. Melody closed her eyes and breathed deeply. A pastry chef's morning typically started before the crack of dawn to make sure the bakery was fully stocked for the breakfast crowd. These early morning walks with Smudge were like a little moment of Zen for Melody. Soon a line would form outside the front door, not only for her signature croissants and cupcakes but also to see Smudge. The little Frenchie had become quite a star in Decadently Delicious. In fact, the citizens of Port Warren were also quite fond of Melody. Despite past events, the bakery's sales were growing steadily, and it was known as one of the more popular spots in Port Warren.

At the sound of a car horn, Smudge barked excitedly. Melody turned. The sheriff of Port Warren, also Melody's fiancé, rolled down his patrol car window as he pulled into an open parking spot in front of the bakery.

"Good morning, my Sweet and Smudge." He cut the engine and exited the vehicle before greeting them properly. "Smudge, what's that in your ear?" Smudge's ears perked up as her brow wrinkled. Alvin squatted down to get a better look. He moved his hand toward her left ear, then pulled it back quickly. Like a magician, Alvin made a treat appear from Smudge's ear! Smudge barked twice as her ears perked up, and she licked her lips. Then, she quickly sat, waiting obediently for the treat. Alvin tossed it to her.

"Where did you learn that trick, Sheriff Hennessey?" Melody looked impressed by his sleight of hand. Smudge crunched the tasty treat.

"One of the deputies taught it to me. I figured it may come in handy sometime." He laughed as he moved in to give Melody a tender kiss. The sweet kiss left Melody's lips tingling. "Did you finish your cake version of Smudge?" he asked as he pulled his lips from hers reluctantly.

Melody offered him a confident smile. "Yes! It's a perfect replica right down to Smudge's smudge," Melody said as she pointed to the mark on Smudge's back. "But I do need a taste-tester. How would you like some Smudge cake for dessert?"

"I would love some!" Alvin gave Melody a squeeze. "I'm sure it's as sweet as the real one." Smudge made soft snuffling sounds as she rubbed against his ankles. These two loved each other nearly as much as Smudge and Melody loved each other. Watching them together, Melody knew Alvin was the right man to complete their family.

"I'm going to take my muse for a quick walk and let her burn off some energy," Melody said. "You know something, Al? Ever since I've had Smudge, I've been more creative and inspired in the bakery. I bet we win that contest."

"I know what you mean, Mel. She's special. Her crime-solving skills have certainly made my job easier," he said with a wink that sent a warm shiver down Melody's spine. Melody loved the little crinkle that appeared in the corner of Alvin's eye whenever he winked. He sure was handsome.

Smudge barked in agreement. She was quite the little sleuth. Alvin's radio crackled, "Sheriff, you're needed over at the hardware store. Looks like some kids caused a little mischief last night." Alvin pressed the button on the side of the receiver. "Headed over there now." Then, Alvin turned to Melody. "Can't wait to see you two tonight. I'm making your favorite." He placed a soft kiss on Melody's cheek.

Melody leaned into the kiss, inhaling a whiff of Alvin's aftershave. She loved the way he smelled just as much as she loved the smell of baked goods in the morning. He smelled like the ocean in the morning. She knew that smell well as she kept one of his sweaters at her place. Whenever she missed Alvin, she wore it to feel close to him. "Of course! I'm looking forward to it," she said.

Alvin pulled back from Melody and looked down at Smudge, who sat staring up at him. Her ears were perked up, high on her head. Her bottom teeth showed ever so slightly. She appeared as if she was waiting for Alvin to kiss her goodbye, too. Alvin couldn't resist, so he squatted down one more time and kissed her on her head. "And I expect you to be at dinner, too, little lady." His finger touched her wet nose playfully.

Smudge, of course, confirmed her attendance with a quick yip. Smudge never missed a dinner.

Alvin returned to his patrol car and headed toward the hardware store. Melody waved as he drove. Once Alvin was out of sight, Melody tugged Smudge's leash. "Let's go this way, Smudge."

Together, they walked up Main Street taking in the early morning sights. It was a beautiful morning, and the townspeople buzzed along the street, appearing cheerful about the spring weather. The florist set up a cart filled with various colored flowers near the front door. The owner of the bookstore swept some stray leaves away from his front door whistling an upbeat tune. He waved to Melody and Smudge as they passed.

Just past the bookstore, Melody noticed a woman standing on a ladder in front of the old Port Warren Animal Shelter. She appeared to be trying to hang a large wooden sign over the front door without any help. Smudge also noticed the woman. Her little wet nose twitched as she sniffed the air. Not recognizing her, Smudge pointed her body in the direction of the woman and tugged her leash gently to get Melody's attention. She wanted to investigate!

"Yep! Let's go check her out, Smudge."

You can read this cute cozy mystery for free when you join my newsletter here

To be the first to find out when Rosie releases a new book and to hear about other sweet romance authors join the exclusive SweetBookHub readers club here.

Strawberries and Sweet Lies

Brides and Blades

The Murder and the Masterpiece

The Poison in the Pie

Silent Night and Deadly Flight

The Beating After the Ball

If you enjoyed this book, Rosie would appreciate it if you
left a review on Amazon or Goodreads.

This little bundle of Frenchie love would appreciate it too,
this is Lila, also known as Piggy Pig.